Ulrich Renz · Marc Robi

The Wild Swans

قوهای وحشی

Bilingual picture book based on a fairy tale by

Hans Christian Andersen

Translation:

Ludwig Blohm, Pete Savill (English)

Jahan Mortezai (Persian, Farsi, Dari)

 Download audiobook at:

www.sefa-bilingual.com/mp3

Password for free access:

English: **WSEN1423**

Persian, Farsi, Dari: **WSFA1510**

Once upon a time there were twelve royal children –
eleven brothers and one older sister, Elisa. They lived
happily in a beautiful castle.

یکی بود، یکی نبود. همه بودند و هیچ کس نبود.

روزی روزگاری دوازده شاهزاده بودند، یازده برادر و یک خواهر
بزرگتر به اسم الیزه. آنها خوشبخت در قصر باشکوهی زندگی
می‌کردند.

One day the mother died, and some time later the king married again. The new wife, however, was an evil witch. She turned the eleven princes into swans and sent them far away to a distant land beyond the large forest.

روزی از روزها مادرشان از دنیا رفت و مدتی بعد پادشاه دوباره ازدواج کرد. همسر جدید پادشاه اما جادوگر بدجنسی بود. او یازده شاهزاده را با جادو به شکل قو در آورد و به جایی دوردست فرستاد، به سرزمینی نا آشنا آنسوی جنگل‌های انبوه.

She dressed the girl in rags and smeared an ointment onto her face that turned her so ugly, that even her own father no longer recognized her and chased her out of the castle. Elisa ran into the dark forest.

او لباس‌های ژنده ای بر تن دخترک کرد و صورتش را با روغنی چنان زشت کرد که حتا پدرش هم او را نشناخت و از قصر بیرونش کرد. الیزه به جنگل تاریک گریخت.

Now she was all alone, and longed for her missing brothers from the depths of her soul. As the evening came, she made herself a bed of moss under the trees.

اکنون او تنهای تنها بود و دلتنگی و غم زیادی برای دیدار برادران گمشده اش داشت. غروب که فرا رسید، زیر درخت‌ها برای خودش بستری از خزه ساخت.

The next morning she came to a calm lake and was shocked when she saw her reflection in it. But once she had washed, she was the most beautiful princess under the sun.

صبح روز بعد کنار برکه ای که رسید، از دیدن چهره خود در آب وحشت زده شد. اما بعد از شستن خودش، دوباره زیباترین شاهزاده خانمی شد که خورشید تا بحال دیده بود.

After many days Elisa reached the great sea. Eleven swan feathers were bobbing on the waves.

بعد از چندین روز الیزه به دریای پهناوری رسید. روی امواج، یازده پرقو مثل اَلاکلنگ بالا و پایین می‌رفتند.

As the sun set, there was a swooshing noise in the air and eleven wild swans landed on the water. Elisa immediately recognized her enchanted brothers. They spoke swan language and because of this she could not understand them.

خورشید که غروب کرد، زمزمه ای در هوا پیچید و یازده قوی وحشی روی
آب فرود آمدند. الیزه بی درنگ برادران جادو شده اش را شناخت. اما چون
آنها به زبان قوها صحبت می‌کردند، او نمی‌توانست حرفهای آنها را بفهمد.

During the day the swans flew away, and at night the siblings snuggled up together in a cave.

One night Elisa had a strange dream: Her mother told her how she could release her brothers from the spell. She should knit shirts from stinging nettles and throw one over each of the swans. Until then, however, she was not allowed to speak a word, or else her brothers would die.
Elisa set to work immediately. Although her hands were burning as if they were on fire, she carried on knitting tirelessly.

در طول روز قوها به پرواز در می آمدند و شبها را کنار خواهرشان در غاری بسر می‌بردند.

شبی الیزه خواب عجیبی دید: مادرش به او گفت که چگونه می تواند برادرانش را نجات بدهد. او می‌بایستی از گزنه برای هر یک از قوها پیراهنی ببافد و روی تک تک آنها بیندازد. در این مدت اما او نباید حتا یک کلمه حرف بزند، وگرنه این باعث مرگ آنها خواهد شد.
الیزه بی درنگ شروع به کار کرد. هرچند دستانش چون آتش می‌سوختند، اما او همچنان خستگی ناپذیر می‌بافت.

One day hunting horns sounded in the distance. A prince came riding along with his entourage and he soon stood in front of her. As they looked into each other's eyes, they fell in love.

روزی از در دوردست‌ها آواز شیپور شکار می‌آمد. شهزاده ای با همراهانش سوار بر اسب آمد و کمی بعد مقابل او ایستاد. لحظه ای آن دو در چشمان یکدیگر خیره شدند و یک دل نه صد دل عاشق یکدیگر شدند.

The prince lifted Elisa onto his
horse and rode to his castle with
her.

شاهزاده الیزه را بر اسب خود نشاند و با
هم به سوی قصرش تاختند.

The mighty treasurer was anything but pleased with the arrival of the silent beauty. His own daughter was meant to become the prince's bride.

خزانه دار مقتدر از آمدن زیباروی بی زبان خوشحال نبود. چون قرار بود دختر خودش عروس شاهزاده شود.

Elisa had not forgotten her brothers. Every evening she continued working on the shirts. One night she went out to the cemetery to gather fresh nettles. While doing so she was secretly watched by the treasurer.

الیزه برادرانش را فراموش نکرده بود. هر غروب بافتن پیراهن‌ها را ادامه می‌داد. شبی به مقصد قبرستان بیرون رفت که گزنه‌های تازه بیاورد. درحالیکه خزانه‌دار مخفیانه او را تعقیب می‌کرد.

As soon as the prince was away on a hunting trip, the treasurer had Elisa thrown into the dungeon. He claimed that she was a witch who met with other witches at night.

زمانی که شاهزاده برای شکار بیرون رفته بود، خزانه‌دار دستور داد که الیزه را در سیاهچال بیاندازند. او ادعا می‌کرد، الیزه جادوگری است که شبها با جادوگرهای دیگر دیدار می‌کند.

At dawn, Elisa was fetched by the guards. She was going to be burned to death at the marketplace.

سحرگاه الیزه توسط نگهبانان آورده شد. او می‌بایستی در میدان شهر سوزانده شود.

No sooner had she arrived there, when suddenly eleven white swans came flying towards her. Elisa quickly threw a shirt over each of them. Shortly thereafter all her brothers stood before her in human form. Only the smallest, whose shirt had not been quite finished, still had a wing in place of one arm.

او هنوز به آنجا نرسیده بود که یازده قوی سفید پروازکنان سررسیدند. الیزه بی درنگ روی هر یک لباسی از گزنه انداخت. لحظه ای بعد برادرانش به شکل آدم مقابلش ایستادند. تنها برادر کوچکتر که لباسش کامل بافته نشده بود، بجای یک دست یک بال را هنوز حفظ کرده بود.

The siblings' joyous hugging and kissing hadn't yet finished as the prince returned. At last Elisa could explain everything to him. The prince had the evil treasurer thrown into the dungeon. And after that the wedding was celebrated for seven days.

And they all lived happily ever after.

روبوسی و دلداری خواهر و برادران هنوز تمام نشده بود که شاهزاده بازگشت. و اینجا بود که الیزه بالاخره توانست کل ماجرا را برایش توضیح دهد. شاهزاده دستور داد خزانه‌دار بدذات را به سیاهچال بیندازند. سپس هفت شبانه روز به جشن و پایکوبی عروسی پرداختند.

و اگر عمرشان بسر نرسیده باشد، هنوز به خوبی و خوشی زندگی می‌کنند.

Children's Books for the Global Village

Ever more children are born away from their parents' home countries, and are balancing between the languages of their mother, their father, their grandparents, and their peers. Our bilingual books are meant to help bridge the language divides that cross more and more families, neighborhoods and kindergartens in the globalized world.

The Wild Swans also propose to you:

Sleep Tight, Little Wolf

▶ A heart-warming bedtime story for sleepy children (and their sleepy parents)

▶ Reading age 2 and up

▶ Available in more than 60 languages

www.childrens-books-bilingual.com

NEW! Little Wolf in Sign Language

Home	Authors	Little Wolf	About

Bilingual Children's Books - in any language you want

Welcome to Little Wolf's Language Wizard!

Just choose the two languages in which you want to read to your children:

Language 1:

French ⌄

Language 2:

Icelandic ⌄

Go!

Learn more about our bilingual books at www.childrens-books-bilingual.com. At the heart of this website you will find what we call our "Language Wizard". It contains more than 60 languages and any of their bilingual combinations: Just select, in a simple drop-down-menu, the two languages in which you'd like to read "Little Wolf" or "The Wild Swans" to your child – and the book is instantly made available, ready for order as an ebook download or as a printed edition.

Hans Christian Andersen was born in the Danish city of Odense in 1805, and died in 1875 in Copenhagen. He gained world fame with his fairy-tales such as "The Little Mermaid", "The Emperor's New Clothes" and "The Ugly Duckling". The tale at hand, "The Wild Swans", was first published in 1838. It has been translated into more than one hundred languages and adapted for a wide range of media including theater, film and musical.

Ulrich Renz was born in Stuttgart, Germany, in 1960. After studying French literature in Paris he graduated from medical school in Lübeck and worked as head of a scientific publishing company. He is now a writer of non-fiction books as well as children's fiction books. www.ulrichrenz.de

Marc Robitzky, born in 1973, studied at the Technical School of Art in Hamburg and the Academy of Visual Arts in Frankfurt. He works as a freelance illustrator and communication designer in Aschaffenburg (Germany). www.robitzky.eu

© 2017 by Sefa Verlag Kirsten Bödeker, Lübeck, Germany
www.sefa-verlag.de

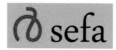

Database: Paul Bödeker, München, Germany
Font: Noto

ISBN: 9783739959016

Version: 20170510

Made in United States
Orlando, FL
17 January 2022

13634005R00018